FOR SEBASTIAN

www.mascotbooks.com

I Can Be A Superhero

For more information, please contact:
Mascot Books
560 Herndon Parkway #120
Herndon, VA 20170
info@mascotbooks.com

Library of Congress Control Number: 2015917084

CPSIA Code: PRT1115A
ISBN-13: 978-1-63177-467-6

Printed in the United States

I CAN BE A
SUPERHERO

written by **Fiona Smart**

illustrated by **Andy Wilson**

Once there was a little girl
whose head was full of pretty brown curls.
She loved to play with all of her toys
like most little girls and boys.

She kept them all in a big wooden box
her teddies, balls and building blocks.
It was decorated with blue and red stripes
with trinkets of all different colors and types.

She would open the lid and take a peek
and imagine her toys playing hide and seek.
Her magical world would come alive
as she counted one, two, three, four, five!

The little girl enjoyed dressing up as
lots of different things.
Characters with hats, capes, magic
wands and multi-coloured wings.
She dressed up her dolls, her toys,
and her teddies
and sang her favorite songs while she
got them all ready.

One morning she jumped up and sang,
"I can be a clown fish in the sea and splish splash all day."

"I can be a kangaroo who bounces up, up and away."

"I can be an astronaut and fly my rocket to the moon.".

"I can be a hummingbird and sing my favourite tune.
I can be whatever I want to be, yes I can,
if I close my eyes and imagine that's really who I am."

"I can be a superhero with a mission to save the world.

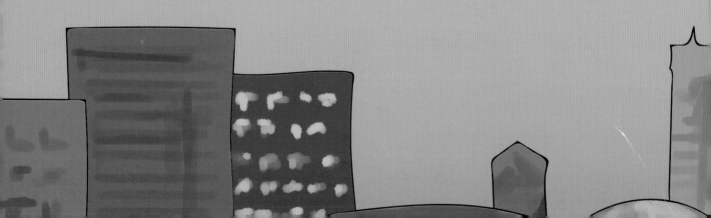

I can be a dancer on stage and twist and spin and twirl."

"I can be a sailor in a boat and sail upon the waves.
I can be an explorer and search for treasure in caves.
I can be whatever I want to be, yes I can,
if I close my eyes and imagine that's really who I am."

"I can be a pilot of a plane and fly around the sky.
I can be an acrobat somersaulting and jumping high."

"I can be a lioness, just listen to my roar.

I can be a deep sea diver exploring the ocean floor.
I can be whatever I want to be, yes I can,
If I close my eyes and imagine that's really who I am."

The little girl's younger brother wanted to join in the fun.
So together they ran around the garden enjoying the sun.

Jumping on the trampoline and taking turns on the swing,
The little girl rode her bike with a bell that
chimed ting-a-ling.

Dressed as a princess and as a
fireman, the two of them would play,
Sharing their toys and teddies until it
was time to tidy away.

When nighttime came, her mommy
tucked the little girl in bed.
She read her favourite story while the
little girl cuddled Ted.

She smiled up at her mommy and said,
"It is fun pretending what I can be,
BUT who I love being the most, is ME!"

About the Author

Fiona was born and raised in London. She studied Art History at university and now resides in Brooklyn, New York. Previously, she lived in Sydney, Australia with her husband Oliver and their young daughter Sienna, where she was inspired to write this story.

Her love of poetry and rhyme started at a very young age. She still remembers the first poem she ever memorised as a little girl. Influenced by the lively imagination of her daughter Sienna and their love of reading countless stories together, Fiona wanted to encourage other children to explore their own make-believe worlds using the best tool they have—their imagination.

Fiona is also a singer/songwriter and enjoys turning her stories into songs. She also loves to travel, has a passion for interior design and fashion, and has big aspirations to become a superhero.

To download the official song, "I can be a Superhero," please visit: www.FionaSmartBooks.com.